LAKE CLASSICS

*Great American
Short Stories III*

Rebecca Harding
DAVIS

Stories retold by C.D. Buchanan
Illustrated by James Balkovek

LAKE EDUCATION
Belmont, California

LAKE CLASSICS

Great American Short Stories I

Washington Irving, Nathaniel Hawthorne, Mark Twain, Bret Harte, Edgar Allan Poe, Kate Chopin, Willa Cather, Sarah Orne Jewett, Sherwood Anderson, Charles W. Chesnutt

Great American Short Stories II

Herman Melville, Stephen Crane, Ambrose Bierce, Jack London, Edith Wharton, Charlotte Perkins Gilman, Frank R. Stockton, Hamlin Garland, O. Henry, Richard Harding Davis

Great American Short Stories III

Thomas Bailey Aldrich, Irvin S. Cobb, Rebecca Harding Davis, Theodore Dreiser, Alice Dunbar-Nelson, Edna Ferber, Mary Wilkins Freeman, Henry James, Ring Lardner, Wilbur Daniel Steele

Great British and Irish Short Stories

Arthur Conan Doyle, Saki (H. H. Munro), Rudyard Kipling, Katherine Mansfield, Thomas Hardy, E. M. Forster, Robert Louis Stevenson, H. G. Wells, John Galsworthy, James Joyce

Great Short Stories from Around the World

Guy de Maupassant, Anton Chekhov, Leo Tolstoy, Selma Lagerlöf, Alphonse Daudet, Mori Ogwai, Leopoldo Alas, Rabindranath Tagore, Fyodor Dostoevsky, Honoré de Balzac

Cover and Text Designer: Diann Abbott

Library of Congress Catalog Number: 95-76747
ISBN 1-56103-065-1
Printed in the United States of America
1 9 8 7 6 5 4 3 2 1

CONTENTS

❧ Lake Classic Short Stories ❧

> *"The universe is made of stories, not atoms."*
> —Muriel Rukeyser

> *"The story's about you."*
> —Horace

Everyone loves a good story. It is hard to think of a friendlier introduction to classic literature. For one thing, short stories are *short*—quick to get into and easy to finish. Of all the literary forms, the short story is the least intimidating and the most approachable.

Great literature is an important part of our human heritage. In the belief that this heritage belongs to everyone, *Lake Classic Short Stories* are adapted for today's readers. Lengthy sentences and paragraphs are shortened. Archaic words are replaced. Modern punctuation and spellings are used. Many of the longer stories are abridged. In all the stories, painstaking care has been taken to preserve the author's unique voice.

Lake Classic Short Stories have something for everyone. The hundreds of stories in the collection cover a broad terrain of themes, story types, and styles. Literary merit was a deciding factor in story selection. But no story was included unless it was as enjoyable as it was instructive. And special priority was given to stories that shine light on the human condition.

Each book in the *Lake Classic Short Stories* is devoted to the work of a single author. Little-known stories of merit are included with famous old favorites. Taken as a whole, the collected authors and stories make up a rich and diverse sampler of the story-teller's art.

Lake Classic Short Stories guarantee a great reading experience. Readers who look for common interests, concerns, and experiences are sure to find them. Readers who bring their own gifts of perception and appreciation to the stories will be doubly rewarded.

🌿 Rebecca Harding Davis 🌿
(1831–1910)

About the Author

Rebecca Harding was born in 1831 in Pennsylvania. Although her family often moved around, she spent most of her life in Philadelphia. Nearly all of Rebecca's education came from her own reading. She began to write early, but her work received little attention until she was 30.

In 1861, *Atlantic Monthly* magazine published her story "Life in the Iron Mills." This realistic tale described the hard lives of industrial workers.

Rebecca quickly became well-known as a "muckraker"—an author who brings society's problems to the attention of the public. In other words, she was someone who stirred up trouble. In her later fiction she dealt with the social injustice faced by black Americans and with political corruption.

At the age of 32, Rebecca married Lemuel Clarke Davis. Marriage brought new conflict into her life. She had trouble balancing her work as a writer and the duties that society expected of a good wife and mother.

This conflict brought on a four-month mental breakdown. Rebecca's doctor advised her to give up writing. One year after her breakdown, however, she published "A Wife's Story." It is the tale of an opera composer and singer named Hattie who struggles to balance her career with her family responsibilities. Hattie has a nightmare in which she loses both her career and her husband. Though Rebecca continued her writing, her character Hattie gave up her work and devoted herself to her home life.

Rebecca Harding Davis had a large family. One of her sons, Richard Harding Davis, followed the same path as his mother. For many years he was a well-known journalist and fiction writer.

Anne

Is it possible to turn back the clock? In this touching story, a middle-aged woman tries to recapture a lost dream. What happens when she wakes up?

THE YOUNG GIRL WITHIN HER WAS STILL BEAUTIFUL. WHY DID THE MIRROR SHOW HER A WRINKLED-SKINNED OLD WOMAN?

Anne

It was a strange thing. In Anne's orderly life, such mysteries were rare. Later she tried to make sense of it. She had fallen asleep out of doors. Well . . . perhaps there are strange forces at work out of doors, both good and evil. These forces do not enter into the boxes in which we cage ourselves. One of these forces may have had her in its grasp.

When Anne fell asleep, she was sitting in a hammock on her porch. The damp sea-breeze blew around her. There were some red roses in her hands. She held them to her cheek, catching their perfume. Sleepily, she thought that the color of the roses and her cheek must be the same. Anne was a great beauty, and happy about it. She had a wonderful singing voice, too. Her songs seemed to rise up into the very sky.

Was that George coming across the lawn? And Theresa with him? She felt a sharp wrench in her heart.

What was Theresa to George, anyway? She was ugly, stupid, and older than he. The woman had nothing to win him. Nothing but money. She did not have cheeks like roses. Nor did she have a voice that could sing at heaven's gate. Anne smiled and slept. A soft warm touch seemed to fall on her lips.

"George!" she cried out. Then she felt a hand on her arm.

"Good gracious, Mrs. Palmer!" said Jane. "I've been huntin' you high and low! Here you are, sleepin' out of doors! The coal man is here, wantin' his money."

Anne staggered to her feet.

"Mother," called a stout young man from the path below. "I must hurry off to the train now. Jenny will be over for tea."

The damp sea-air still blew gently across the porch. The crushed red roses lay on the floor.

But she—

There was a mirror in the living room. Going up to it, Anne saw a stout woman of 50. Her hair was gray and she had a big nose. Her cheeks were pale.

Anne opened her mouth to sing. But all that came out was an awful yawp. Then she remembered. She had lost her voice after an illness when she was 18. She put her trembling hand to her lips.

George had never kissed those hands. He had married Theresa more than 30 years ago. Now George Forbes was a famous poet and author.

Her fingers still lay upon her lips. "But I was so sure that he—" she whispered. She felt a shudder of shame, yet at the same time, her soul flamed. Something within her cried out, "I am here—Anne! I am beautiful and young. If this old throat were different, my voice would ring through earth and heaven."

"Mrs. Palmer, the coal man . . ."

"Yes, I am coming, Jane." She took her checkbook and went down to the kitchen.

When she came back she found her daughter Susan at the sewing machine. Mrs. Palmer stopped beside her, smiling sadly. Susan was so young! Surely, she would be interested in this thing that had moved her mother so deeply. It must have been some force outside of nature that came over her just now. Her life had been turned back to its beginnings!

"I fell asleep out on the porch a while ago, Susy," she said. "I dreamed I was 16 again. It was very real. Even now I cannot shake off the impression that I am still young and beautiful and in love."

"Ah, yes! Poor dear papa!" Susy said. She sighed and snipped her thread. She wanted to be kind. She wanted to say something sympathetic about the ancient love of her parents. But really, it seemed a little ridiculous. Besides, she was in a hurry to finish sewing the ruffle. Jasper was coming up for tea.

Mrs. Palmer went on upstairs, feeling

chilled and defeated. She had been sure
Susy would understand. How could she
explain to the girl that she hadn't
dreamed of her poor dead papa? After all,
it wasn't quite right for a respectable,
middle-aged woman to have such a
dream. Her pale cheeks reddened as she
shut herself in her room. She had been
very foolish to tell Susy about it at all.

Mrs. Anne Palmer was always in awe
of her children's hard common sense.
They were both Palmers. When James
was just a baby, his mother had shrunk
from his calm, attentive gaze. "I shall
never be as old as he is already," she had
thought. But as the children grew up,
they loved their mother dearly. Her
devotion to them would have touched
hearts of stone. And the Palmers were
not stony-hearted, really. They were
good-humored folk, like their father.

After her husband's death, Mrs.
Palmer had managed the plantation.
And she had done so with great energy
and success. She had followed her
husband's habits. She was exact and

careful in both peach-growing and management. She had paid all the debts on the property, and then invested in western land. Mrs. Palmer had made herself and the children rich. She was respected as a woman with a man's mind.

But James and Susan were mostly amused by their mother. They didn't understand the admiration the other planters felt for her. Of course, she was the dearest woman in the world. But she had no head for business!

True, she had her peach crops, her land holdings, and her bank stock. But did those things prove adult good sense? They were only dear mamma's lucky hits. How could an intelligent woman grow so bored with pleasant church activities? Why did she refuse to go to the delightful Literary Circle? And hadn't she once gone all the way to Philadelphia to hear a strolling singer?

Neither of her children could quite understand such childish outbreaks. All a Palmer needed was a good peach farm, a comfortable house, and servants to worry about. What else *was* there? Their mother should have been very happy.

Susy saw that her mother was very uneasy today. When a letter came from Pierce and Wall, her peach sellers in Philadelphia, she threw it down unopened. It didn't seem to matter that she had shipped them 300 crates of peaches last Monday. She didn't even seem to care.

Usually she was a most careful housekeeper, keeping a sharp eye on the help. But she disappeared for hours this afternoon, even though Jasper Tyrrell was coming for tea. Jane was sure to make a greasy mess of the soup if she was left to herself.

Jasper certainly had paid attention to Susy lately. But she knew that he was a cool, careful young fellow. He would look at the matter on every side before he committed himself. The Tyrrells were an old, well-to-do family. They wanted perfection from his bride.

"Greasy soup has often disgusted a man," thought Susy. "Every detail is very important right now."

Just before sunset Mrs. Palmer came up the road. Her hands were full of brilliant maple leaves. Susy hurried to meet and kiss her. The Palmer family showed affection by constantly petting and buzzing about each other. The entire household worried if a draft blew on mamma's neck or if the baby had a cold. But just now Mrs. Palmer was bored by this habit of constant watchfulness.

"No, my shoes are *not* damp, Susy. No, I did not need a shawl. I'm not in my old age, child. Good heavens, you'd think I was on the verge of the grave!"

"Oh, no, but you are not young, darling mamma," Susy said. "You are just at the age when illness can set in if you're not careful. Where were you?"

"I took a walk in the woods," Mrs. Palmer said.

"*Woods!* No wonder your shoulders are damp," Susy said. "Come in right now, dear. Drink a hot lemonade and go to bed. Walking in the woods! Really, now, that is something I cannot understand." She smiled at her mother as though she were a small, foolish child. "To go wandering about in the woods for no earthly reason—" She stopped herself, adding, "Here, I'll press those leaves for you."

"No. I don't like to see pressed leaves and grasses in vases," her mother said. "When summer is dead, let it die." She threw down the leaves impatiently, and the wind blew them away.

"How odd mamma is!" Susy thought. "So little self control!" Then she said aloud, "It is nearly time for Mr. Tyrrell to be here. Can Jane manage the soup?"

"Oh, I suppose so," said Mrs. Palmer, casually. She picked up a book.

Anne was somewhat cold and distant all evening. Peter clattered the dishes as he waited at the supper table. The tea was lukewarm. Jasper was lukewarm too, silent and critical.

James's wife, Jenny, had come over for supper. It had upset her to find her mother-in-law Anne so distant. So she chattered about the baby. Jasper, bored and uneasy, shuffled in his chair. He had always thought Mrs. Palmer was a charming hostess. Usually she was full of care for everyone. But tonight she seemed blind and deaf to everything.

Susy gave her mother an angry look. Was she trying to ruin everything?

"How silly these children are!" Mrs. Palmer thought to herself. "How cautious and unromantic Tyrrell was in his courting. Susy, too. It seemed that she thought only about Tyrrell's income."

At 17 *her* horizon had not been so cramped! How wide and beautiful the world had been then! Nature had known her and talked to her. Music had always spoken to her, as well. And when love and romance came along—Mrs. Palmer felt a pleasant chill.

She sat silently until they got up from the table. Then she hurried to her own room. This creature within her—this Anne—was still beautiful and loving. Why did the mirror show her an old wrinkled-skinned woman?

She *ought* to think of that old long-ago self as dead. But it was *not* dead!

"If I had only married the man I loved," her heart cried out. "Then I should have had my true life. *He* would have understood me."

How ridiculous and wicked it all was!

"But I was a loyal, loving wife to Job Palmer," she told herself. She lit the lamp and faced the stout figure in the mirror. "In many ways, my life went down into the grave with his."

But then she saw the gray eyes flash in the mirror. Yes! They were Anne's eyes—and young Anne had never been Job Palmer's wife.

Mrs. Palmer did not go downstairs again that night. This quiet hour was usually the happiest of the day. James and Jenny always came in to kiss her goodbye. Sometimes Susy came in to read with her mother a bit before tucking her snugly into bed.

But tonight Mrs. Palmer locked her door. She wanted to be alone. She tried to read, but soon pushed the books away. How unbearable this clumsy old body had grown to her!

Two years ago when she was ill, it semed that she suddenly had become 80 years old! Yet now the blood of a 16-year-old was rushing through her veins! How strange.

By morning she had made an odd decision. *She would go away.* Why shouldn't she begin somewhere else, and live out her own life? Why shouldn't she enjoy music and art and the companionship of thinkers and scholars? Her face grew pale as she named these things so long forbidden to her.

She put on a traveling dress. Then she placed a few things in a bag. She made sure to take her checkbook.

"Carry this to the station," she said to Peter. Half asleep, he was making up the morning fires.

"Are you going to Philadelphy today, Mis' Palmer? Does Mis' Susy know?" he asked with a worried look.

"No. Just tell her I've been suddenly called away," she said.

She smiled as she walked to the station. Susy would think she had gone away on business. She would look to see if her mother had taken her overshoes and jacket. "I hate overshoes! I would like to tear that jacket to bits!" Anne thought, as she took her seat on the train. Yes, she was going to escape from it all. She would no longer be watched like a helpless old lady. Then the train moved. She was free! At last she could be herself.

First she would go to the trust company in Philadelphia. She would take her bonds from the vaults. The children had their own property—they were secure without her.

Where should she go? To Rome? Venice? No. There were just too many Americans trotting around Europe. She must be rid of them all. There was Egypt and the Nile River. What about Iceland? That would be another world up there. There would be no peaches or church activities or village gossip.

"I want to meet people who are searching for truth and beauty. There must be people who never stoop to gossip or fuss over money-making," she thought. She remembered the wonderful words of George Forbes's last poem. "If only I had been his wife," she thought to herself. "I too might have thought great thoughts and lived a noble life."

She tried to thrust away this idea. In her heart she did not mean to be a traitor to her dead husband. She had loved him well and long.

But the passion of her youth was maddening her thinking. Her husband Job had been a good, commonplace man. But this other one was a man of great insight. To her he seemed to be a dictator of thought to the world.

Now the train rolled into the Broad Street station. Mrs. Palmer went to the trust company and withdrew her bonds. She had never visited the city alone before. In the past, Susy always came along to "take care of dear mamma." Susy had her own ideas as to "what people in our position should do," of course. She always took her mother to the best hotel and ordered a costly dinner.

Today Mrs. Palmer went to a cheap little cafe in a back street. She ate a simple broiled chop. The delight she felt was like that of a runaway dog, chewing on a stolen bone. As she stepped into the street a cold rain began to fall. Damp and chilled, she returned to the station.

Where should she go? Italy or the Nile—oh, no! There were people she knew! The Crotons from Dover were getting out of the train. She must hide herself at once. Afterward she could decide on her travels. She got in line at the ticket window.

"Boston?" said the agent.

Mrs. Palmer nodded. In five minutes she was seated in a parlor car. The train thundered across the bridge above a huge cattle yard. Looking down on the cattle in their sheds, she felt uneasy. "I wonder if Peter will give Rosy her warm mash tonight," she thought to herself.

Only three seats in the car were occupied. Two men and a lady came in together. They sat near Mrs. Palmer. She could not help hearing their talk.

"You might open up your window, Corvill," said one of the men. "Unless Mrs. Ames is afraid of getting cold."

Corvill? Ames? Mrs. Palmer half rose from her seat. Why, Corvill was the name of the great artist. She had a painting of his called "Hagar." She never looked at the face in that portrait without a wrench at her heart. All human pain and longing spoke in that woman's face. The same human feelings that spoke in George Forbes's poems. And Mrs. Palmer knew who Mrs. Ames was, too. She was a famous writer on social problems.

There had been a conference in Philadelphia, Mrs. Palmer remembered. Many well-known authors and artists had attended. No doubt these two famous folk had been there. Mrs. Palmer drew nearer. She felt as if she were creeping up on the immortals. A thrill went through her. This was what could happen when peaches and soup and servants were left behind!

"Oh, open the window!" said Mrs. Ames to Corvill. She had a hoarse voice that came in deep gusts and snorts. "Let us have some air! The sight of those foreigners huddled in the station made me quite ill. Women and babies—all skin and bone and rags."

But Mrs. Palmer had almost wept over that poor group. That sick baby's cry would wring any woman's heart, she thought. Could it be that this great lover of humanity had no feeling for the masses? But there was the man who painted "Hagar." Surely *he* would show pity and tenderness—wouldn't he?

"I'm sorry they annoyed you," he was saying. "There were some very good subjects among them. Look, I made two sketches." He pulled out a notebook. "That half-starved woman near the door—see? Fine line in the chin and jaw. I wanted a dying baby for my painting, 'Exiles,' too. I caught the very effect I wanted in that sick child."

Mrs. Palmer turned her head away. Perhaps it was a small disappointment, but it hurt her. These people were just *peddlers* in art and humanity. They were not on the high pure level of truth and beauty. They weren't on the level where George Forbes stood, for instance.

Mr. Corvill was talking about the decoration of the passenger car. "Not bad at all," he said, looking around. "There is great tenderness in the color of that ceiling. And just look at the lines of the chairs! They are full of feeling."

Mrs. Palmer listened, puzzled. But now the two famous people were looking at the landscape. If he found feeling in the legs of a chair, what new meanings would he not discover in nature? Outside the window lay a vast stretch of lonely marsh. Mrs. Palmer could see narrow black lagoons creeping across it.

"Nice effect," said Mr. Corvill. "I like that moss on the barn against the green. I find very few things worth using this fall, however. Too much brown."

How could it be, she wondered. Had these people traded off humanity for art? Had they lost sight of beauty's highest meaning?

Corvill turned to the other man. "I

should think you could find material for some verses in these flats. You know— *The Land of Sorrow*. Something in that line. Eh, Forbes?"

Forbes! Her breath stopped. That fat hunched man with the greasy black whiskers? Yes, that was his voice. When had it become so arrogant?

"Oh, I've stopped verse-writing," he said. "There's no market for poetry. My publishers shut down on verses more than five years ago."

Then Forbes turned, and she saw his face clearly. He had thin hard lips and cold eyes. Was this man *her* "George"? Or had *that* George never lived—except in her imagination?

"Mr. Forbes." She rose. The very life in her seemed to stop. Her knees shook. But habit is strong. She bowed as she said his name. He looked at her and saw a courteous, well-bred old lady. Yet some power in her gray eyes startled him. It brought him to his feet.

"I think I knew you long ago," s e said. "If it is you—?"

"Forbes is my name, ma'am. Lord bless me! You can't be—but there's something familiar in your eyes. You remind me of Judge Sinclair's daughter, Fanny."

"Anne was my name."

"Anne! To be sure. I knew it was Nanny or Fanny. I ought to remember—I had a crush on you for a week or two. You know you were the best catch in the county, eh? Sit down, ma'am, sit down."

"Is—your wife with you?"

"You refer to the *first* Mrs. Forbes— Theresa Stone? Oh, I have been married twice since her death. I am now a widower."

Suddenly Job Palmer seemed to stand before her. In memory she could see his fine clear-cut face and friendly eyes. He knew little outside of his farm, perhaps. But how clean his soul was! And how truly he had loved her!

At that moment the car swayed sharply from side to side. The lamps went out. "Hello!" shouted Forbes into the darkness. "Something is wrong! We must get out of this!" He rushed to the door. She grabbed onto her chair.

Then a huge weight fell on the car, crushing in the roof. Mrs. Palmer was jammed between two beams. She was unhurt, but she fainted at the shock.

In half an hour she was cut out and laid down on the riverbank. She was wet and half frozen, but her bones were whole. She tried to rise, but could not. Every joint ached. Her gown was in shreds. The mud was deep under her, and the rain pelted down. In her mind she saw the fire burning on her hearth at home. The easy-chair in front of it welcomed her.

Then some men with lanterns came up and bent over her. "Great God, Mother!" one of them cried. It was James. She had no idea he had been on the same train. He was on his way to New York for a business meeting.

The next day she was safe in her own bed. The fire in her room was burning brightly. Susy was keeping guard. Jenny had just fed her a bowl of delicious soup. The baby had fallen asleep in her arms.

James came in on tiptoe. He bent over his mother anxiously. She saw all of them through her half-shut eyes.

"My own family!" she thought. She thanked God for the love that kept her warm and safe.

As she dozed, Susy and James bent over her. "Where on earth could she have been going?" said Susy.

"To New York," James said. "No doubt to make a better contract than the one she has with Pierce and Wall. To make a few more dollars for us. Or maybe she was seeing about an investment. Her bonds were all in her bag. Poor, dear, unselfish soul! Don't worry her with questions, Susy—don't speak of it."

"No, no, I won't, Jim," said Susy, wiping her eyes. "She's suffered enough."

* * *

One day when his mother was quite well, James spoke to her about the day of the accident. "We had a famous fellow-traveler on that train to New York, Mother. It was Forbes, the author."

"A most disagreeable, common person!" said Mrs. Palmer. " Don't take any notice of such people, James. He is just a shopman of literature."

* * *

Susy married Jasper Tyrrell that winter. They live in the homestead now, and Mrs. Palmer has four grandchildren. She spoils them to her heart's content while Jasper and Susy manage the farm. In most every way she has a quiet, easy, happy life. Yet sometimes a certain note of music or the wail of the wind brings a strange expression into her eyes. Her children do not understand it.

At such times Mrs. Palmer will say to herself, "Poor Anne!" as if remembering a loved one who died long ago.

But *is* she dead? she wonders. And if she is dead here—will she ever live again?

At the Station

Would you wait 20 long years for a loved one's return? Aunt Dilly did just that. Was it a mistake to believe in her brother?

FOR THE FIRST TIME THE CONDUCTOR COULD SEE THAT
JUDSON WAS HANDCUFFED.

At the Station

There was nothing special about Miss Dilly's little corner of the world. It was a wayside inn in North Carolina. The little town, called Sevier Station, lay next to the railroad track. Besides the inn, there were two or three unpainted houses. Beyond were swampy tobacco fields stretching into the pine woods.

Nothing was special about Miss Dilly either. She was a pudgy old woman of 60. Her shapeless body was covered by a plain blue dress. A big white apron was usually tied about her waist. She had a face like a baby. Her round, innocent blue eyes were the friendliest in the world. Most days she wore a snowy white handkerchief pinned about her neck and another one tied over her ears. This was to soothe her mysterious pain. The mountaineers thought they knew what it was. They said someone had looked at her with an evil eye.

"They tell me it must be so," Miss Dilly would say. "But, of course, my dear, it happened by accident. *Nobody* would hurt a person that way—on purpose."

Miss Dilly had had this pain only since she had lived at the inn. She was born in the mountains—up on the Old Black. She thought that if she could go back there, she would be cured. But her younger brother, James, owned this farm and the inn. When their mother died 20 years ago, he let Preston Barr take over the property. The agreement was that Preston—the "Squire"—would live there, rent free. In return, he would give Dilly a home and the money made from one field of tobacco every year. Then James had set off West to make his fortune. At first his letters came regularly. But it was ten years now since she'd last heard from him.

When the pain came on, nobody ever heard a groan from Miss Dilly. She would shut herself up in her room and stay there. Something like a funeral gloom would hang over the whole clearing then.

When the attack was over, Miss Dilly would come out, pale but smiling. Then she would shake hands with everyone as if she had come back from a long journey. Squire Barr would always try to be helpful. He'd say, "Aunt Dilly, I know you want to go back to yer home on the Old Black. If that would give you ease—then say the word. But what we'd do without you, I don't know!"

Then Mrs. Missouri Barr would look at Miss Dilly. Tears would roll down her thin cheeks. The girls would hang about Miss Dilly, patting her hands. Colonel Royall would declare that "the whole clearin' had been powerful interrupted while you was gone."

These were the happiest moments of

Miss Dilly's happy life. For about the thousandth time she would explain, "It seems to me if I was in the old place, I'd get young again and lose this pain. But then, what would James think when he came back here? What if he were ready to carry me to his home in Colorado? Me *gone*—after my promise to wait? And to leave all of you—Preston, that would be too hard!"

At other times, life at Sevier Station was quiet. Miss Dilly spent most of her time sewing or knitting. From her window she could see the six men of the village smoking and talking. All the village children ran in and out of her room. Miss Dilly told them Bible stories.

There was no church near the station. Miss Dilly, with her Bible, was the only preacher known to these people.

Every day in the morning the train passed the station. It was going to the mountains. In the afternoon it came down. Each time it stopped for five or ten minutes. When the train came in sight, the six men, the women, children, pigs, and chickens waited, breathless. Miss Dilly was always by the window to see it go by. If only she could ride on the train just once! Only for a mile! This was the one secret ambition of her life.

Sometimes the train was late. Then it would stop for the passengers to take supper. The excitement in the tiny town rose to fever height whenever this happened. Mrs. Barr and the girls were busy. Miss Dilly took a strong interest in the passengers. She nursed the babies, gave candy to the children, poured a drink for the tired, dusty women.

All the passengers seemed to love Miss Dilly. They treated her with tender respect. But then they boarded the train again and were swept out of sight. Every time, Miss Dilly would stand waving with tears in her eyes.

"The dear friends hardly come till they go away again," she would say.

One stormy night in winter the train was delayed in the mountains for two hours. One of the passengers' children had fallen ill. The train was stopped, and a man with healing powers was sent for. The passengers were in no hurry. In those days, nobody in Carolina was ever in a hurry. Everybody was anxious to help the baby.

Two men in the railroad car did not join the group around the sick child. They sat on a back seat. Then the dark, middle-aged one stooped forward, listening.

"Poor little kid!" he said, sincerely. "I had a boy once. He only lived to be seven. If that little fellow had lived, he'd have made his mark on the world!"

"Died at seven?" said Captain Foulke, his companion. "So sorry, Mr. Judson."

Judson dropped back in his seat and said no more.

By this time the sick child was asleep. The train rushed along through the gathering twilight. Judson glanced out the window with a strange look on his face.

"Isn't that the old Sevier plantation?" he asked.

"Yes, sir. It's changed a good bit since

they built the railroad."

"There was a house just beyond here. It used to belong to a family named Holmes," Judson said.

"Yes. The railroad built the station right next to it. The old Holmes house is an inn now. Squire Barr's the owner."

"Any of the Holmeses still livin' there?" asked Judson.

Captain Foulke turned and looked at him curiously. "Miss Dilly," he answered. "She lives with the Squire and his family. James Holmes, her brother, went West years ago. I hear he's made a fortune out there. Folks hereabouts still think a lot of him, though."

"Do they?" asked Judson.

"A friend of yours?" asked the Captain.

Judson stared out into the darkening fields. "No. He was no friend of mine," he said at last.

Then the engine gave a shriek. The conductor got up, yawning. "Sevier Station, gentlemen," he said. "Train stops here for supper."

The passengers slowly made their way

off the train. Judson stiffened in his seat.

"My God! I can't get out here!" he said. "There are folks in that house that know me." He panted with terror. Foulke and the conductor stood over him anxiously. For the first time the conductor saw that Judson was handcuffed.

Foulke explained in a whisper. "I'm bringin' him to Raleigh from Tennessee. He's to stand trial for manslaughter. But you can see that he's a high-toned gentleman—he's made no trouble."

"Come, come, Mr. Judson," said the conductor. "Captain Foulke must have his supper. So must you." He wrapped a large blanket around the prisoner and pulled his hat over his brow. "Your own wife wouldn't know you now, sir. Come now. You can sit in the parlor if you don't care to take supper."

Judson hesitated. He looked at the lighted windows of the inn. Both terror and longing flickered in his eyes.

"I'll go," he said, getting up. "And I'll not try to escape, so help me God."

* * *

Miss Dilly brought a cup of tea to the man in the parlor. "I'm so sorry you're feelin' poorly, sir," she said. "Won't you take this, just to warm you?"

"No," said the man, gruffly. The lamplight sparkled in her kind blue eyes.

"Don't go," said Judson. "Stay with me a few minutes. I'll never see you again."

Something in his voice startled her. Then, collecting herself, she sat down.

"That's just what I always say to myself," she said. "Folks come here and stay just long enough to make friends. Then they go, and I never see them again."

"And you're satisfied with that?" sneered Judson.

Miss Dilly drew herself up.

"Why, they're my friends, as I said. But I have my own family, sir."

"Who are they?" he asked softly.

"There's my brother, James Holmes. I'm waitin' here for him right now. I'm expectin' him every day. And there's my

father and mother. They're up on the Old
Black. And there's my brother's son. He
was just seven when he—went away."
Tears crept down her withered cheeks.

"And you think your brother will be
coming soon?"

"I *know* it," said Miss Dilly, quietly.
"Every day since he went away I've asked
the Lord to send him back. So he—*has
to come*. What I've thought I'd like—" She
hesitated.

"What?"

"If we could go back, just the two of
us, to our house on the Old Black. Maybe
him and me could live there together a
few years—"

The man's head dropped on his chest.
She jumped to her feet, afraid that he
was ill. "I'll bring you something—" She
laid her hand on his arm.

Just then the passengers came in from
supper. The conductor and Captain
Foulke thrust themselves between the
prisoner and Miss Dilly. They talked
loudly, bustling about him, keeping her
from seeing the iron handcuffs. The

passengers crowded out the door.

Judson motioned the men aside. "I must speak a word to that woman." He walked over to Miss Dilly.

"Don't ever get tired praying for your brother," he said. "For God's sake, don't get tired! And maybe he *can* come back!"

When the train was gone, Miss Dilly went about her work. She prayed for her brother that night as she had never prayed before. She didn't know just why she did it. "Lord, bring him back to me," she cried.

* * *

After that night, the people at the station noticed a change in Miss Dilly. She had always been kind. But now she was tender to every living thing she could reach. She had always been cheerful. But now she was breathlessly anxious to make everyone happy.

"I guess she's gettin' ready for the end," said Colonel Royall.

Everybody whispered about it. They kept an anxious watch on Miss Dilly. At last Mrs. Barr told her what they feared.

Miss Dilly laughed a sound, healthy laugh.

"It's not *death* at all that's comin'," she said. "It's James! The Lord will send my brother back to me. I think of it all the time. If one of you is sick, I think—what if it was James? And I try to help you. And if another one of you is sad, I think, what if that was James? And I try to cheer you up. That's the truth, Missouri. It isn't death, it's James."

Summer came, and then winter, and then summer again. Two years went by.

Judson had stood trial. He'd been convicted and served his term in prison.

On the day of his release, he spoke with the warden of the prison. "There's a woman, sir, who has made a different man of me," Judson said. "She has loved me and believed in me all my life. She's tied me to God with her prayers. From now on I'm goin' to trust to her and God to pull me through!"

"Take your own name back again, Judson," the warden told him. "Say nothing to this woman of your past life. Start over someplace where your name isn't known. Now good luck and may God bless you, sir."

This was in October.

Christmas that year brought its usual stir of excitement to the inn. Fancy foods were ready the day before Christmas. Father Ruggles, the traveling minister, was coming down from the mountains for Christmas dinner. He arrived at noon. "I don't like Miss Dilly's looks," he said to the Squire. "Old age, eh?"

"Not a bit of it," replied Preston. "It's her brother James. She's tired out from waiting on that man. These last two years she's been expecting him every day. She watches the train every night and morning."

The men looked out at Miss Dilly. She stood in the yard, feeding the chickens. Across the road came Mr. Nutt, the carpenter. He kept the post office, too.

"Mail is in, gentlemen," he called. "Two circulars and this letter. For Miss Dilly."

The Squire handed Miss Dilly the

letter without saying a word to her.

"For me! A letter! For—?"

She could hardly breathe when she saw the writing on the envelope. She went straight to her own room.

The news spread. In ten minutes the whole little town had gathered. They waited breathlessly.

At last Miss Dilly came out. Her face was shining with peace.

"James has gone back to our house on the Old Black," she said in a quiet voice. "Him and me is to live there together. He's comin' tonight on the train."

Nobody spoke. The news took their breath away.

"He'll stay here a week, to see his old friends," she said. "But look—there's the train!" Then she broke down and began to cry. The women gathered about her and cried along with her.

The men rushed to meet the train.

"What a great day tomorrow will be!" said Squire Barr. "I hope the turkeys will hold out!"

Colonel Royall spoke out next. His

voice shook with feeling. "God almighty has sent Miss Dilly her Christmas gift! Here's the train, gentlemen!"

It rolled up the track and stopped. A short, heavyset man came out on the platform. He had gray hair and a nice kind face.

"That's him! That's James!" shouted the Colonel.

Then they all broke into a cheer. They pressed round him, waving their hats and shaking his hand.

"She's up there, James," said the Squire. "Go right away, sir. She's been waiting a long time."

The End of the Vendetta

Two Southern families have been feuding for 100 years. Now a decision has to be made. What will it cost to end the vendetta?

"You can't go to Otoga. The yellow fever is there. Six people died yesterday."

The End of the Vendetta

It was the second day of Lucy Coyt's journey. Every mile of railroad track took her farther from home. For years she had looked forward to this—finally she was setting out to earn her living. She was on her way to the mysterious South.

At that time—before the Civil War— the South was like a foreign land to most Northerners. Families like Lucy's often trained their daughters as teachers. Then they sent them to the cotton states—the South—where they could earn a better living than they could working at home.

Their families also hoped they might end up with husbands. In fact, a gold mine could open up in the shape of a young planter. Some of Miss Coyt's classmates had met their husbands this way. She imagined them ruling over an army of servants. Naturally she dreamed of such a fate for herself.

But Lucy Coyt knew it was wrong to hold slaves. At least that was her belief now. It had been ever since David Pettit had talked to her about it the other evening. As a brand new minister, David had brought some strange new ideas back from divinity school.

"No one must suspect that he's an abolitionist," thought Lucy. "He'll wait a long time for a job in our church if they find out." The abolitionists believed that all slaves should be freed. Many people did not agree.

She leaned back. It was too bad that she couldn't have stayed to watch over him. She could have helped poor David have a better chance. Then suddenly the train lurched to a stop.

Miss Coyt looked out the window. On the riverbank below the bridge lay a hunched heap. It was dressed in gray flannel and yellow cotton. The men from the train ran toward it. "Something's wrong. I'd better take hold at once," thought Miss Coyt. She took her purse out of her bag and put it in her pocket. She then hurried out after the men. Lucy believed that women were better then men in any emergency. At home, she was always the one who pulled her father and brothers along.

Now she reached the quivering heap on the bank. It was a woman. Miss Coyt kneeled down and lifted her head. The gray hair was clotted with blood. "Why, the poor old thing!" cried Lucy.

"It's old Mis' Crocker!" said a train man. "Her cabin is nearby. I seen her on the bridge. I guess she heard the train comin' and she jumped, and—"

"Don't stand there chattering. Go for a doctor!" cried Miss Coyt.

"I'm a doctor, ma'am," said one of the passengers, quietly. He stooped to examine the woman. "She's not dead. Not even hurt much. Looks like her arm is broken."

The men carried Mrs. Crocker to her cabin. Holding the woman's hand, Lucy went along. The other women watched from the car window. They were just as sorry as Lucy. But they were Southern women. It was their habit to leave great emergencies in the hands of men.

"What does that bold girl think she's doing?" they said to each other. "The gentlemen will attend to it."

The men saw Mrs. Crocker open her eyes. So they straggled back to the train.

"Time's up, doctor!" shouted out the conductor. "The express is due here in two minutes."

The doctor was cutting away Mrs. Crocker's flannel sleeve. "I need bandages," he said. Lucy quickly looked around the bare little cabin. She saw a pillow cover and tore it into strips. The doctor dressed the arm as calmly as if he had the whole day to do it. Miss Coyt kept her eye on the puffing engine. All the clothes she had in the world were in her trunk on that train. What dawdlers these Virginians were! There! The train was moving! She could not leave the woman—but her clothes!

In a puff of steam, the train shot into the hills. The doctor fastened his last bandage. Miss Coyt rushed to the door. For the first time, the doctor looked at her. Then he quickly took off his hat.

"Don't be alarmed," he said.

"But the train is gone!"

"You have your ticket? There will be another train before nightfall. You will find your trunks waiting for you at Abingdon."

"Oh, thank you!" gasped Lucy. Suddenly she felt ashamed of her fearful feelings. "It was very silly of me. But I never traveled alone before."

The doctor had heard about Northern women. He supposed that they were always sure of themselves. Now his calm eyes rested on Miss Coyt as he folded his pocketbook.

"It was my fault that you were delayed,

madam," he said. "If you will permit me,
I will look after your luggage when we
reach Abingdon."

Lucy thanked him again. How lucky
she was to meet this kind doctor. Then
she turned to help Mrs. Crocker, who was
struggling to her feet.

Mrs. Crocker went out to the doctor.
He was sitting on the log which served
as a step. She looked at the bridge.

"Mighty big fall that were," she said.
"Not another woman in Wythe County
could have done it without breakin' her
neck."

"Ah, you have another 20 good years
of life in you yet, Mother," he laughed.
He glanced at her muscular arms. Wind
and sun had tanned her skin to a fine
leather color.

"Oh, I'm tough enough," she said. "I
brought up 11 children right here.
They're all gone now—dead or married.
I helped build this house with my own
hands. Ploughed and hoed every hill of
that corn."

"It's outrageous!" said Lucy. "At your

age a woman's children should support
her. I would advise you to give up the
house at once. Divide your time among
your children. You should rest."

"Oh, no, missy. I never was one for
jaunting around. I was born here 70
years ago. I reckon I'll make an end
here."

"Seventy years!—*here*?" thought Lucy.
Her eyes wandered over the corn, the pig-
pen, the old cabin. The doctor watched
her with an amused smile. Mrs. Crocker
went in to stir the fire.

"Better, you think, not to live at all?"
he asked Lucy.

"I would hardly call this living," she
said. "I've seen it often on farms. Feeding
pigs and children until both were big
enough to be sent away. But for 70 years!
It is no better than the life of that fat
worm over there."

The doctor laughed. He put his hand
down for the worm to crawl over. "Poor
old woman! Poor worm!" he said. "There's
nothing as merciless as a woman like
you. Would you leave nothing alive that's

not young and beautiful as you are? You should reconsider. The world was not made for kings and queens alone. You must leave room in it for old women, and worms, and country doctors."

Lucy laughed, but she said nothing. She didn't quite understand this country gentleman. She pointed to the worm.

"I don't know how you can touch that awful thing," she said. "It creeps up into your hand as if it knew that you were on its side."

"It *does* know," the doctor said. "If I wanted it for bait, it would not come near me. I believe that all creatures know their friends. Watch for a moment."

The doctor walked a few steps into the edge of the woods. Then he threw himself down in the deep grass. Soon a bird came circling down and perched beside him. Another followed and then another.

"Have you a magic charm?" she asked.

"No. But I've been friends with the animals since I was a child. They know it. Even as a baby, I didn't find anything alive to be unfriendly. But madam, I beg your pardon! I didn't mean to bore you with the story of my childhood."

"*Bore* me! Why, I never met anyone with such an odd quality before!"

Miss Coyt now believed that this man had not only great intelligence, but also goodness. What life and strength he could carry to the sick and dying! It was like the healing power of the old saints.

Now she had lots of questions. Was he married? Was he a church member? Lucy was neither engaged nor in love. She *intended* to be in love some day—but only when the right man passed all her tests.

The doctor had no interest in her, however. When Mrs. Crocker asked Lucy about herself, he did not listen. He whistled to the farm dog instead.

"What are you doin' here in Virginia, anyhow?" Mrs. Crocker asked.

"I came from Pennsylvania to teach school," said Lucy. "I'm going to a place called Otoga. It's in Carolina."

"You have some friends or family in these parts, I reckon?"

"No, none at all," Lucy said. "Unless I

may call you one, Mrs. Crocker." Lucy laughed nervously.

"I reckon you won't see much more of me, ma'am," Mrs. Crocker answered. "Otoga, hey? My son Orlando lives there. I'd keep away from that town if I were a young woman alone. Orlan's told me a heap about it."

"Why, what's the matter with Otoga? I *must* go there. My work at the school—"

"Matter? Nothin'—only it's there the Van Cleves have gone to live. You've heard of them, I reckon."

"The Van Cleves?" Lucy asked.

The doctor came up to the open door with his watch in hand. "The train is due in 20 minutes," he said.

"I'm ready," Lucy said. "But tell me, who are these people, Mrs. Crocker? I must live among them."

"They won't hurt *you*, I reckon," the old woman said. "There's no higher toned people than the Van Cleves and the Suydams. Only it's sort of unpleasant where they are, sometimes." She lit her pipe, in no hurry to continue.

"You see, those two families swore death against each other nearly 100 years ago. Since then not one of the men on either side has died peacefully.

"There's only one Suydam left, and that's Colonel Abram. His father was shot by the Van Cleves. There's just one Van Cleve left, and he is livin' in Otoga. But Colonel Abram will track him down sooner or later. He'll shoot him, just like he shot his brother."

"But is there no law at all in Otoga?" cried Lucy. "I can't believe such a crime would go unpunished anywhere."

The doctor tapped on the window. "The train is in sight. You must bid our friend good-bye."

Lucy quickly shook hands with the old woman and hurried to the train.

* * *

Three days later Lucy was rumbling along the mountainside in an old wagon. Suddenly a dozen weather-beaten houses came into view.

"Yonder is Otoga," said the driver.

"Hi, Dumfort!" shouted a man's voice. "Hold on there!" A big young fellow stepped out of the brush. "You can't go to Otoga. The yellow fever is there. Six men dead since yesterday mornin'."

Dumfort pulled up his mules. "*Six!*" he exclaimed. "That's half the town!"

"So I say," the young fellow went on. "My wife and I have been on the lookout for you since mornin'."

Lucy peeped out of the wagon. She could see the bold, pink-cheeked face of the young countryman. He stood pulling at his red beard and frowning with regret for his neighbors.

"Well, I've got the mail here—and a passenger, too," said Dumfort. "What am I supposed to do?"

"The mail will keep. Drive up to my house. My wife will give you and the other man a bed for the night."

"It's not another man," Dumfort said.

The young man stepped forward quickly. His manner changed instantly. He jerked off his quilted wide-rimmed hat. Lucy thought that his wife must have made that hat out of an old dress.

"I didn't know there was a *lady* inside," he said. "Sorry I was so rough with my news. Come on up to my house now. My wife will tell you there's no danger."

"I shall be very glad to go," Miss Coyt said to the driver.

Dumfort drove up a rough mountain road. He stopped before a log cabin that was plainly the first modest home of two poor young people. Hurrying in from the field came a plump, freckled young woman. She held a baby in her arms.

"Now, Dorcas, let's have supper," the farmer said to his wife. "Our friends must be as hungry as bears."

Dorcas smiled and began to fry chicken. Lucy suddenly remembered that she needed to find a place to stay.

"What would you charge for board?" Lucy asked her hostess. "Perhaps I could stay here just until the sickness is over in Otoga. That is, if your charges are reasonable." Her rule was always to make her bargain before buying. That way she was never cheated.

The woman's fair face burned red. "We *don't* take folks in to *board*," she said in her sweet voice. She looked at Lucy curiously. "It's mighty lonesome here on the mountains. But we'll take it as *very* kind of you if you want to stay."

"It is you who are kind," said Lucy. She felt miserably small and almost cruel. But how could she have known? In her hometown, they didn't treat strangers so generously.

When the baby awoke, Lucy picked him up. Suddenly, she felt very lonely and far from home.

"What do you call him?" she asked.

"His real name is Humpty," said the young mother. "But he was baptized Alexander. Alexander Van Cleve."

Lucy sprang to her feet. "*Van Cleve!*" she cried, staring at the farmer. "I thought your name was Thomas?"

"Thomas Van Cleve," the man said. "Why? What's wrong with that?"

Lucy felt as if a blow had been struck at her. "They told me in Virginia that the Suydams were on your track."

There was a sudden silence. Miss Coyt stumbled on. "I didn't expect to come in your way. I'm not used to such things—and this poor baby! It's a Van Cleve too!"

The young man took the baby. "Quiet yourself. Humpty will not be hurt by—anyone." He put the baby on his shoulder and walked down to the chicken-yard. Without a word, his wife went in and shut the door. "I see that I've made a mistake," Lucy said to Dumfort.

"Yes. But you couldn't be expected to know," he said. "I never heard a Suydam's name mentioned out loud to a Van Cleve before. It was so surprising, it didn't seem *decent* somehow."

"Well, I don't quite understand why," groaned Lucy.

"No? Well, there's some things that aren't ever talked about. Now this family's got a—a discussion—hanging on with the Suydams for 100 years. And—well, probably you're the first person ever to mention it to them."

The next morning Thomas Van Cleve set off by daylight, whistling behind his steers. Before noon he came back up the mountain. But now his head hung low. His face was silent and grim.

Dorcas ran down the path to meet him. "Are you sick, Tom?"

"No."

"Have you . . ." she glanced swiftly around. "Have you *heard* something?"

"Nothing. But I thought it best to give up work for today," he said.

Dumfort came to Lucy. "Thomas has had a warnin'," he said, in a low tone. "Colonel Abram is on his track."

Lucy tightened her arms around Humpty. "He's coming *here*?"

"I think so. But Thomas ain't seen him yet. He's been warned. I've heard that Van Cleves can always tell when a Suydam is near."

"Nonsense!" Lucy set the child down.

Van Cleve came into the house. "Dorcas, bring Humpty in," he said quietly. "Stay indoors today." Then he went up into the loft, closing the trap-door behind him. Lucy thought she could hear the click of a gun.

"He's loading his gun up! Suydam is comin'!" Dumfort exclaimed. Then he whispered to Lucy, "Thomas ain't the same man he was this mornin'. Now he's layin', and waitin'."

"To murder another man!" Lucy cried. "And to think that he had family prayers this morning!"

"What's that got to do with it?" Dumfort demanded. "Thomas has his duty laid out. He's got his brother's murderer to punish. The law has left it to those two families to settle with each other. The Suydams have blood to avenge!" In a minute Van Cleve came down from the loft and seated himself. His face was turned toward the road that led up to the house.

Lucy felt as if she couldn't draw her breath. The air seemed full of death. "Well, I'll be first to meet the wolf," she said aloud, laughing nervously as she set off down the road.

As she came nearer to the creek she heard a horse crossing. She tried to cry out, but her mouth would not make a sound. When the horse and rider came into sight, she laughed wildly.

It was the good-humored doctor. At her cry, he turned quietly, and smiled calmly. He tied his horse and came over to her.

"You look frightened. What are you afraid of, Miss Coyt?"

She poured out the whole story.

"I saw nobody," he said calmly.

"It's a vendetta," she began.

"You shouldn't get too excited by the mountain gossip," he interrupted, gently. "But I must reach Otoga before noon."

"But yellow fever is there! Half the population is dead."

"Worse than that, I'm afraid," he said, gravely. "We heard this morning that there's no doctor now. And for two days there's been no nurse, nor anybody to bury the dead."

"You're going to help them?" she asked.

"I'm a doctor," he said simply. "I know how to nurse. If worse comes to worse, I can dig a grave. Now I must ride on. But first I will take you safely home. Where are you staying?"

"At the cabin yonder. Behind the pines. Thomas Van Cleve's place."

"Young Van Cleve lives in that cabin?" the doctor asked.

"Yes, with his wife and child."

"A child? Is it a boy?" he asked.

"Yes, the dearest little fellow. Why do you ask?" Lucy said.

"It is with Van Cleve I had business to settle. I've been looking for him for a long time."

"Then you will come to the house with me?" she asked.

Lucy stopped. She felt troubled and frightened, but she didn't know why. The man showed not a trace of feelings.

"No, those poor devils in Otoga need me," he went on. "I reckon that it's the right thing to do." Turning around, he mounted his horse. Then he rode down the road and disappeared from sight.

* * *

Four days passed. Dumfort stayed on at the cabin, helping with the work. Sometimes he brought news of Otoga that he got from someone fleeing the fever. One morning he came in and called Van Cleve outside.

"One of them poor wretches fell on the road. He's got the plague. He wants to see you, Thomas. *You*, personally."

"Me? Who is he?"

Dumfort lowered his voice to a quick whisper. "It's him—the man that's been following you and your family, Thomas."

Van Cleve uttered an oath, but it choked on his lips. "And he's dying? What does he want of me now?"

"God knows. I don't." The two men stood silent. "He's been doctorin' them poor souls in Otoga," Dumfort said.

Still Van Cleve did not move. Then, with a jerk, he started downhill. "I'll go to him. Bring those other medicines, Dumfort."

When Van Cleve reached the dying man, though, he saw that it was too late for medicines. He knelt beside him and lifted his head. He motioned for Dumfort to stand back out of hearing.

What words then passed between them no one but God ever knew.

Van Cleve didn't return to the cabin until the sun was setting that day. He was pale and worn out, but he tried to speak cheerfully.

"I'm sorry to be late, Dorcas. Dumfort and I buried a poor fellow that died of the fever. But I'd like you and Miss Coyt to come to the grave. It would seem kinder, somehow." He carried the baby in his arms. When the little group reached the place, he spoke. "Humpty, I wish you'd kneel down on the grave and say your little prayer. I think he'd know and feel better. And—there's another reason."

* * *

The next week Miss Coyt received a letter. With very red cheeks, she told Dorcas that she had to return home immediately. A church had asked Mr. Pettit to work as its minister. His letter asked her to be his wife. This would put an end to any teaching in the South.

In a day or two Dumfort drove her back to Abingdon. The little family in the cabin went back to their quiet life.

Thinking About
the Stories

Anne

1. All the events in a story are arranged in a certain order, or sequence. Tell about one event from the beginning of this story, one from the middle, and one from the end. How are these events related?

2. What period of time is covered in this story—an hour, a week, several years? What role, if any, does time play in the story?

3. Is there a character in this story who makes you think of yourself or someone you know? What did the character say or do to make you think that?

At the Station

1. Who is the main character in this story? Who are one or two of the minor characters? Describe each of these characters in one or two sentences.

2. An author builds the plot around the conflict in a story. In this story, what forces or characters are struggling against each other? How is the conflict finally resolved?

3. Think about the times in which this story is set. What circumstances in the story do not exist today? Why was it important to the Van Cleves and the Suydams to continue feuding for as long as they did?

The End of the Vendetta

1. All stories fit into one or more categories. Is this story serious or funny? Would you call it an adventure, a love story, or a mystery? Is it a character study? Or is it simply a picture the author has painted of a certain time and place? Explain your thinking.

2. In what town, city, or country does this story take place? Is the location important to the story? Why or why not?

3. Are there friends or enemies in this story? Who are they? What forces keep the friends together? Why is it easy for Miss Dilly to make friends? Explain.